JAYDEN'S
IMPOSSIBLE
GARDEN

Mélina Mangal

Illustrated by **Ken Daley**

free spirit
PUBLISHING®

Published by Free Spirit Publishing Inc., 6325 Sandburg Road, Suite 100, Minneapolis, MN 55427, in collaboration with Strive Publishing, 3801 North 27th Avenue, Minneapolis, MN 55422

Library of Congress Cataloging-in-Publication Data
Names: Mangal, Mélina, author. | Daley, Ken, 1976- illustrator.
Title: Jayden's impossible garden / by Mélina Mangal ; illustrated by Ken Daley.
Description: Minneapolis, MN : Free Spirit Publishing Inc., [2021] | Audience: Ages 4–8.
Identifiers: LCCN 2020017120 (print) | LCCN 2020017121 (ebook) | ISBN 9781631985904 (hardcover) | ISBN 9781631985911 (pdf) |
    ISBN 9781631985928 (epub)
Subjects: CYAC: Nature—Fiction. | City and town life—Fiction. | Neighborhoods—Fiction. | Mothers and sons—Fiction. | People with disabilities—Fiction.
Classification: LCC PZ7.1.M36466 Jay 2021 (print) | LCC PZ7.1.M36466 (ebook) | DDC [Fic]—dc23
LC record available at https://lccn.loc.gov/2020017120
LC ebook record available at https://lccn.loc.gov/2020017121

Free Spirit Publishing does not have control over or assume responsibility for author or third-party websites and their content.

Reading Level Grade 2; Interest Level Ages 4–9;
Fountas & Pinnell Guided Reading Level M

Edited by Alison Behnke
Cover and interior design by Shannon Pourciau

10 9 8 7 6 5 4 3
Printed in China
R18860721

Free Spirit Publishing Inc.
6325 Sandburg Road, Suite 100
Minneapolis, MN 55427-3674
(612) 338-2068
help4kids@freespirit.com
freespirit.com

FSC
www.fsc.org
MIX
Paper from
responsible sources
FSC® C144853

Free Spirit offers competitive pricing.
Contact edsales@freespirit.com for pricing information on multiple quantity purchases.

For Sameer, with Love—MM

For C.J. Anything is possible.

Just believe, and you can achieve. —Uncle Ken

Jayden loved nature. At school, he played outside during recess.
On field trips, he pretended to be a scientist,
collecting acorns, stones, and twigs.

In Jayden's favorite books, kids played in treehouses or climbed rocks.

But after school, Jayden had to stay inside.

"There's no nature here in the middle of the city," Mama said.

Jayden *knew* there was. On his way home, he watched squirrels scrounge for snacks. He listened to the calls of cardinals. He felt fat, furry snowflakes as they fell from the sky and landed on his face.

A wheelchair van lowered Mr. Curtis onto the sidewalk in front of Jayden's building each afternoon. He would inch forward and stop, then look around, from the sky to the ground. He'd close his eyes to breathe in the cold fresh air before wheeling in.

Jayden wondered if Mr. Curtis wanted to be outside as much as he did.

Every day Jayden walked home
v-e-r-y s-l-o-w-l-y so
he would get there just as the
wheelchair van pulled up.

He opened the building door wide, and waited as Mr. Curtis wheeled inside.

"Thank you, Jayden," said Mr. Curtis.

Mr. Curtis was outside one day as Jayden walked up.

"What are you looking at?" Jayden asked.

"That crocus," Mr. Curtis said.

"How'd it get there?"
Jayden asked with awe.

"Magic!" Mr. Curtis winked.
"Spring is here."

Jayden smiled, wanting to stay. Then his shoulders slumped.
"I have to go inside. Mama says there's nothing to do out here."

"My daughter says that too!" Mr. Curtis nodded.
"But I just want to be out all day."

"Can I go outside with Mr. Curtis?"
Jayden asked Mama. "He loves nature too!"

"What a kind idea," Mama said. "But Jayden,
there's no nature here in the middle of the city."

From then on, Jayden and Mr. Curtis met every day after school. Mr. Curtis told stories of his childhood adventures in Mississippi. Jayden shared facts he'd found in animal books.

They compared nature collections. They searched for anthills.

They built towers from old boxes, stones, and sticks.

"This is our secret fort," Jayden said.

They planted mystery seeds in old containers.

"This is our magical garden,"
Mr. Curtis said.

One day, Jayden tried to share the secret.

"Mama, here's the magical secret fort garden I made with Mr. Curtis."

"These old buckets and boxes?" Mama shook her head.
"Jayden, honey, I'm glad you and Mr. Curtis are enjoying time together.
But there's no nature here in the middle of the city."

So Jayden and Mr. Curtis made a plan.

"My daughter didn't understand why I wanted her to bring me her empty coffee containers rather than recycling them," Mr. Curtis chuckled.

Jayden helped Mr. Curtis decorate the coffee containers. They planted zinnia, marigold, and nasturtium seeds inside them.

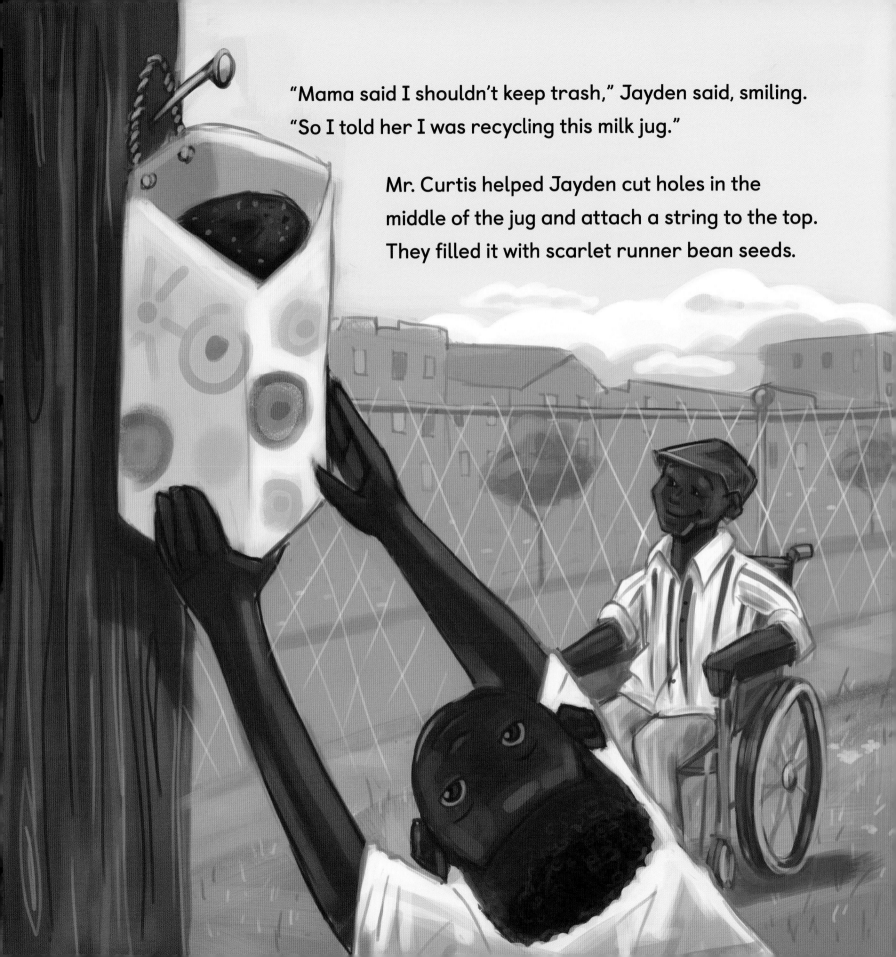

"Mama said I shouldn't keep trash," Jayden said, smiling. "So I told her I was recycling this milk jug."

Mr. Curtis helped Jayden cut holes in the middle of the jug and attach a string to the top. They filled it with scarlet runner bean seeds.

Together they discovered something new each afternoon that summer.
While watering the garden, they plucked a caterpillar and put it in a jar.
It became the guardian of the fort.

After watching a spider weave
its web, Jayden stretched an old
basketball net across the top of his
tower and knotted the bottom. It
became a tiny hammock.

When flowering green vines began
inching along the laundry lines, Mr. Curtis
twirled the tendrils toward the tower.
They became a royal rope bridge.

Jayden was almost ready for the last part of his plan—
showing Mama the magical secret fort garden.

But would she see the garden
the way he and Mr. Curtis did?
Was there enough *nature* to show her?

One hot summer evening, the secret got out.

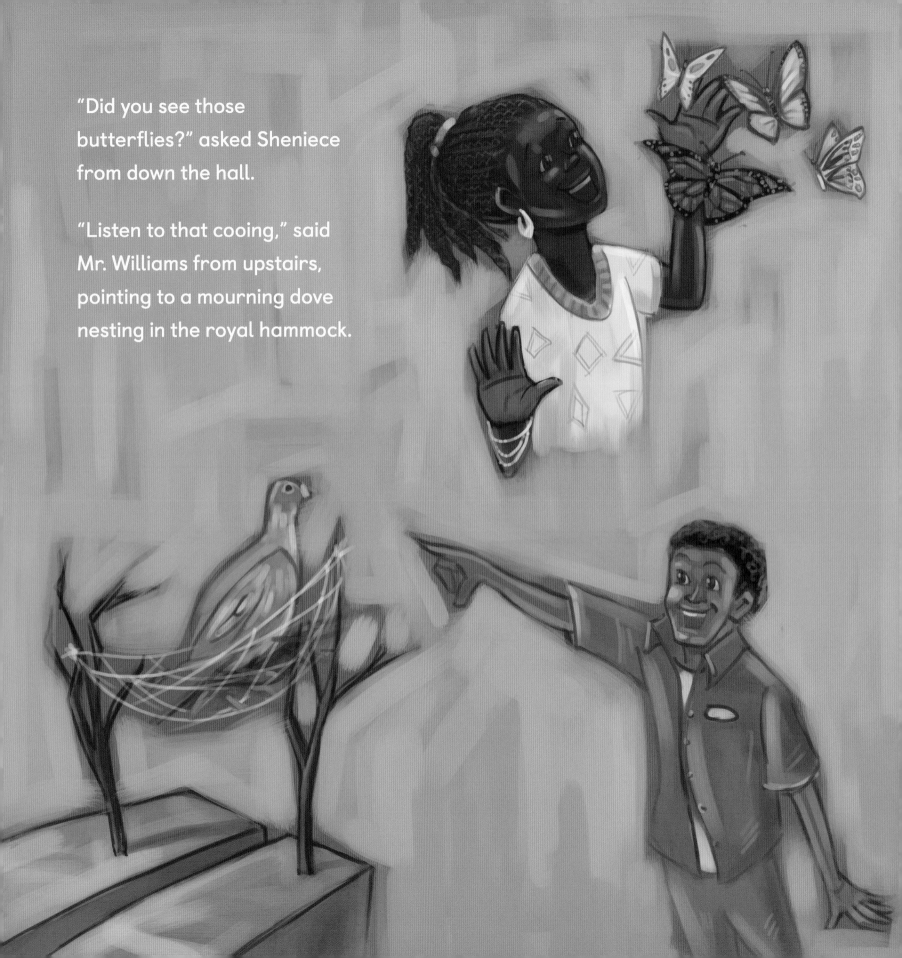

"Did you see those butterflies?" asked Sheniece from down the hall.

"Listen to that cooing," said Mr. Williams from upstairs, pointing to a mourning dove nesting in the royal hammock.

"Look!"

Everyone rushed to the rope bridge.

Mama hurried down the stairs toward the small crowd.
"What's wrong, Jayden?"

"Listen, Mama," Jayden whispered, taking her hand.

"A hummingbird!" Jayden said, pointing.

Mr. Curtis nodded.

Neighbors smiled.

Everyone soaked in the beauty
that surrounded them.

"It's our magical secret fort garden!" Jayden beamed.

This time, Mama saw what Jayden saw.

The magic of nature was all around them—
right there in the middle of the city.

A NOTE FROM THE AUTHOR

When I was very young, my siblings and I were always outside: climbing trees, playing in fields of tall prairie grass, biking, and skipping rocks on the river. Nature was all around me. When I moved to the city, I realized I had to pay closer attention to appreciate the nature that surrounded me.

I still live in a big city, and I make sure to get outside each day, even in the frigid winter and on the hottest summer days. Being out in my neighborhood helps me get to know my human neighbors. It also allows me to observe my *other* neighbors—the ones that crawl, fly, or sprout. The more I observe, the more I understand and appreciate them. Even in the city, birds visit window ledges, plants crawl and climb up walls, and ants build. Noticing the smallest beings around us can give us insight into the wider world. We are just a small part of nature, but we are all connected—just as Jayden, Mama, Mr. Curtis, and their neighbors are connected. We may see neighbors all the time without discovering that we share interests with them. Until we reach out and get to know the people around us, we'll never know how we can enjoy each other's company or how we can help each other.

Look closely at the plants and animals where you live, as Jayden does, and you will notice interesting details and differences. For instance, maybe the same bird visits each day. Can you tell it apart from the other birds in your neighborhood? How does it sound? Practice making the sounds you hear. Or find a tree or other plant outside your window or door. Is it growing in a pot, the yard, a crack in the sidewalk? How does it look in the morning, and again in the evening? Write or draw what you see, including as much detail as you can.

Did You Know?

In this section you'll read about some insects, animals, and plants that may live in your neighborhood. What do you already know about them? What more would you like to learn?

ANTS

Though some people think ants are bothersome, these tiny insects help our environment. They pollinate some plants, help keep the soil healthy, and spread seeds around so plants can grow. For more information on ants, visit AntWeb at antweb.org.

CROCUSES

Crocuses are *nyctinastic* plants. That means that they close their petals at night and open them with the morning sun. For more information on crocuses, visit the website of The Old Farmer's Almanac at almanac.com/plant/crocuses. To learn more about all kinds of plants, go to the Brooklyn Botanic Garden website at bbg.org/news/category/children_families.

HUMMINGBIRDS

Hummingbirds memorize the location of every hummingbird feeder and flower in their path, so they know where to return each year. For more information on hummingbirds, visit hummingbirds.net.

MOURNING DOVES

Both parents, a male and a female, feed young mourning dove hatchlings. Many bird parents drop food into the mouths of their babies. But mourning dove hatchlings get their food themselves by taking it directly from their parents' open beaks. For more information on mourning doves (and many other birds), visit the Cornell Lab website All About Birds at allaboutbirds.org.

SCARLET RUNNER BEANS

Most parts of the scarlet runner bean plant can be eaten. Bees and hummingbirds love to drink nectar from the flowers. Humans can eat the flowers. You can eat the green pods as well, cooking them like green beans. If the pods dry out, the seeds inside can be removed, cooked, and eaten like dried beans. Some people also dig up and eat the roots. For more information on scarlet runner beans, visit the Kids Gardening website at kidsgardening.org/growing-guide-scarlet-runner-beans.

Invite Nature in with Recycled Crafts

These activities will help you bring nature close, wherever you are. Ask an adult to help you, and enjoy observing the birds you feed and the plants you grow.

MAKE A COFFEE CONTAINER PLANTER

Materials

a clean, dry coffee can or plastic container

duct tape, permanent markers, paint, stickers, or other art supplies (optional)

rocks or pebbles (ideally the size of large marbles, but any size will work)

potting soil

seeds for planting (such as sunflower, marigold, radish, or scarlet runner bean seeds)

Directions

Decorate the outside of the coffee container with duct tape, permanent marker, or other art supplies—or just leave it as is. Next, layer the bottom of the can or container with rocks or pebbles for drainage, an inch or two deep. Fill the rest of the container with potting soil. Evenly space seeds on top, leaving a couple of inches between them. Press them gently into the soil, and then water them—just enough to get the soil moist, not so much that water stays on top of the soil. Place the container in a location that gets the right amount of sunlight for your seeds. (You can look online to find out how much sun specific plants need.) Check the pot daily for signs of growth. Make sure to water regularly!

MAKE A MILK JUG BIRD FEEDER

Materials

a clean, dry 1-gallon milk or water jug, with cap

pencil or pen

sharp knife (*Note!* Be sure to have an adult help you with cutting.)

hole puncher

chopstick or thin wooden dowel (this will become a perch for the birds, and should be long enough to go all the way through the jug and stick out on either side)

strong string, yarn, shoelace, ribbon, or plastic fishing or beading line to hang the feeder (about 2 feet long)

permanent markers, paint, or colored duct tape

bird food (sunflower seeds, cracked corn, millet, grain sorghum, peanuts, thistle)

Directions

Draw two large door-like openings on the sides of the jug that are immediately to the left and right of the handle, making the openings as even and level with each other as you can. Have an adult help you cut out the openings with the knife. (When using a knife, always move the blade *away* from your body.) Use the hole punch to make one hole under each opening. Poke the chopstick or dowel in one hole, through the jug, and out the hole on the other side. Now you have a bird perch!

Next, remove the cap and punch four holes around the base of the jug's spout, spacing them as evenly as you can. Lace one long piece of string or line through the four holes. Replace the cap and knot the ends of the string together. Pull up two loops of string that you can hang on a branch or hook. (Having two loops instead of one will help the feeder stay balanced.) Decorate the bird feeder with markers, paint, and tape. Pour bird food into one of the large openings you cut out. Then hang your bird feeder where you can see it, and watch the birds that come. Record which birds visit and how they behave at your feeder. Keep it full, and make sure to clean it out occasionally.

ABOUT THE AUTHOR AND ILLUSTRATOR

Writing at the intersection of nature, literature, and culture, **Mélina Mangal** highlights young people whose voices are rarely heard and the people and places that inspire them to explore their world. She is the author of short stories and biographies for young people, including *The Vast Wonder of the World: Biologist Ernest Everett Just,* winner of the Carter G. Woodson Book Award and named an NCSS/CBC Notable Social Studies Trade Book for Young People. Mélina also works as a school library teacher in Minnesota and enjoys spending time outdoors with her family, whether it's in her backyard or hiking in the woods. Visit her online at melinamangal.com.

Ken Daley is an artist and an award-winning illustrator of two picture books, *Joseph's Big Ride* and *Auntie Luce's Talking Paintings* (which received a Kirkus starred review and an Américas Award Honorable Mention). Ken draws inspiration for his work from his African-Caribbean roots, his life experiences, and the people and cultures he encounters along the way. Ken was born in Cambridge, Ontario, Canada, and he lives with his wife and two pets. You can visit him at kendaleyart.com.

Other Great Books from Free Spirit

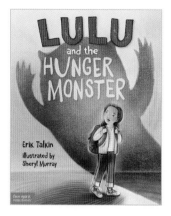

Lulu and the Hunger Monster™
by Erik Talkin, illustrated by Sheryl Murray
For ages 5–9. 40 pp.; HC; full-color; 8" x 10".
Free Leader's Guide freespirit.com/leader

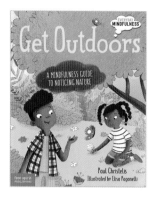

Get Outdoors
A Mindfulness Guide to Noticing Nature
by Paul Christelis, illustrated by Elisa Paganelli
For ages 5–9. 32 pp; HC; full-color; 7½" x 9".
Free Leader's Guide freespirit.com/leader

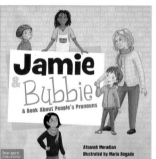

Jamie and Bubbie
A Book About People's Pronouns
by Afsaneh Moradian,
illustrated by Maria Bogade
For ages 4–8. 32 pp.; HC; full-color; 8" x 8".
Free Leader's Guide freespirit.com/leader

Y Is for Yet
A Growth Mindset Alphabet
by Shannon Anderson,
illustrated by Jacob Souva
*For ages 4–8. 40 pp.; HC;
full-color; 8¼" x 9".*

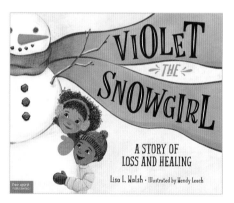

Violet the Snowgirl
A Story of Loss and Healing
by Lisa L. Walsh,
illustrated by Wendy Leach
*For ages 5–10. 36 pp.; HC;
full-color; 11¼" x 9¼".*

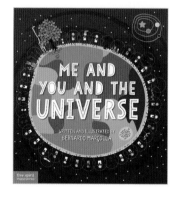

Me and You and the Universe
written and illustrated by Bernardo Marçolla
*For ages 3–8. 36 pp.; HC w/ jacket;
full-color; 8¼" x 9".*

Interested in purchasing multiple quantities and receiving volume discounts?
Contact edsales@freespirit.com or call 1.800.735.7323 and ask for Education Sales.

Many Free Spirit authors are available for speaking engagements, workshops, and keynotes.
Contact speakers@freespirit.com or call 1.800.735.7323.

For pricing information, to place an order, or to request a free catalog, contact:

Free Spirit Publishing Inc.
6325 Sandburg Road • Suite 100 • Minneapolis, MN 55427-3674
toll-free 800.735.7323 • local 612.338.2068 • fax 612.337.5050
help4kids@freespirit.com • freespirit.com